'/14

SAVING SINBAD!

Michael Foreman

For the crew of the St. Ives Lifeboat – past, present and future

Kane/Miller
BOOK PUBLISHERS

You probably think it's fun being a dog,
but a dog's life isn't just running about,
fetching sticks, and rolling over. Some of us
have to work for a living.

I go to work with my master every day.
He doesn't realize how useful I am.
But even when I'm just lying in the shade,
I've always got an eye open, making sure
he is all right, although he thinks I am
asleep. Well, sometimes I *am* asleep,
but then I have an ear open. Honest.

Sometimes the work is dull, but the job
we're doing this week is really great.
My master has got the job of mending the
church roof and fixing a new flagpole on
the tower. The view is fantastic!

From the top of the tower I can see over the roofs of the town
to the harbor, and beyond to the wild sea.
I can see the barman rolling barrels into the pub, the barber brushing
his fat cat's tail, and the butcher's boy whistling down the street on
his bike. I can smell the sausages in his basket.

I can see Johnny the Slater and our builders on the church roof below. I can see the artist in his studio and the old sea captain looking through his spyglass. I can hear singing in the church and a big car with white ribbons is coming down the street.

There are storm clouds on the horizon . . .

"W_{hoosh} . . . . . . BANG!"

The sky is suddenly full of
screaming seagulls.

A second distress rocket bursts
above the bay in a big puff of
smoke. My master has disappeared
down the steps from the tower,
leaving his saw quivering halfway
through a plank of wood,
and I race after him.

Now the town is loud with running feet.
The builders are off the church roof and
racing with the artist, the barber,
the barman and the bridegroom down
the street to the harbor.

The butcher's boy overtakes them on his
bike, a string of sausages trailing from his
basket.

By the time I have hidden the sausages for later, the doors of the Lifeboat House are open and Johnny the Slater has started the engine of the blue tractor. The artist is stripping off his old painty smock, and the sea captain is shouting into the phone.

My master, the builders, the barber, the barman, the butcher's boy and the bridegroom, are all pulling on yellow waterproofs and lifejackets.

This is the life! Running behind the tractor, barking instructions
as it tows the lifeboat down the slipway and across the sands towards
the leaping waves. The tractor swings around, backing the lifeboat into
the wild sea until it floats free of its trailer.

The artist revs the lifeboat's engines and the butcher's boy,
the bridegroom and the builders cling on as the boat plunges
through the breaking waves and out into the bay.

From the end of the pier, I can see
the lifeboat rise and disappear, then
rise again on the giant waves.
In the distance, a mast and tattered
sail mark a sinking sailing boat.

I race around the harbor and out onto the cliff for a better view.
My eyes are full of sea spray and wet fur as the wind whips into
my face but I can see two of the lifeboat crew jumping
into the sinking boat.

Now they are helping a man, a woman and a child up into the lifeboat. But the child is crying, "Sinbad! Sinbad!" and pointing into the water. Someone is missing. There is a roaring overhead and a rescue helicopter joins the search.

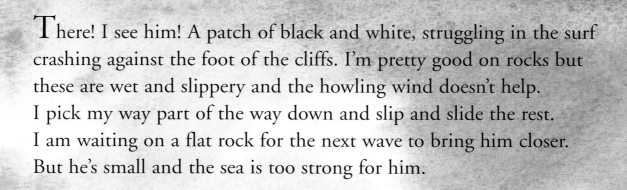

There! I see him! A patch of black and white, struggling in the surf crashing against the foot of the cliffs. I'm pretty good on rocks but these are wet and slippery and the howling wind doesn't help. I pick my way part of the way down and slip and slide the rest. I am waiting on a flat rock for the next wave to bring him closer. But he's small and the sea is too strong for him.

There's nothing for it – I'll have to bring him in myself.

I dive in. Gotcha!
I grab him by the collar and hang on.
The sea is pulling us under, but I won't let it separate us.
Then a wave gathers us up and we are swept onto the rocks.

Before the wave can pull us back into the sea,
I drag the little dog away and we scramble to safety.
Slowly, slowly we start to climb the cliff. The lifeboat crew cheer,
especially my master.

An hour later the storm has passed and I'm back at work.
I can see the builders on the church roof, the bride and groom
posing for photographs, the barber giving his fat cat yet another
saucer of milk and the sea captain having tea with a man and
a woman while a small girl plays on the sand with Sinbad.

I can hear the butcher and the butcher's boy
arguing about the missing sausages . . .

My master looks at me and, for once, I pretend I really am asleep.

First American Edition 2002 by Kane/Miller Book Publishers, La Jolla, California

Originally published in the U.K. by Anderson Press, London

Copyright © 2001 by Michael Foreman

All rights reserved. For information contact:
Kane/Miller Book Publishers
P.O. Box 8515
La Jolla, CA 92038-8515

Library of Congress Control Number: 2002102888

Printed and bound in Italy by Grafiche AZ, Verona

1 2 3 4 5 6 7 8 9 10

ISBN 1-929132-34-4